The Adventures of Johnny Wheeler

A tale of magic and friendship in Hardcastle Craggs

By

Sebastian Darley

Table of Contents

CHAPTER ONE

The wood called Hardcastle Craggs

There's a small village deep in the heart of Yorkshire called Hebden Bridge. And in Hebden Bridge lies a special place called Hardcastle Craggs.

Hardcastle Craggs is a wood full of slick trails and crossing snails, a sparkling river with small flying fishes.

In the spring, the woodland floor is covered in a lavender sea of bluebells in every direction. It's such a serene and idyllic place to wander, with dappled light and the tinkling sound of the river flowing through the heart of the woods.

Several spots of Hardcastle Craggs are perfect for picnics. Especially near the old watermill which had been converted into a small coffee shop with a working water wheel that was popular with tourists.

A short walk down the river is a set of stepping stones that lead to a patch of green grass and a large boulder that children liked to climb on.

Hardcastle Craggs is also home to a very unique group of animals. Animals who are going to invite a young boy to join them on adventures he'd never dreamed of.

CHAPTER TWO

Johnny Wheeler in a world he hates

Johnny Wheeler was a boy dark black hair, large blue eyes, and puffy cheeks. He hated leaving London and his friends.

Johnny had lived all of his nine years in the heart of London's hustle and bustle. As far as he was concerned, moving to a village in the middle of nowhere was... well... they might as well move to the moon!

Johnny didn't care about living in a wood. Even if according to his dad, it would be the best thing to happen in their lives. Living among a bunch of trees was a fate worse than death to Johnny. His life would be over. Trees don't talk, don't honk, don't speed, and never play games. All trees ever do is stand in a spot and wave all day. Now, where's the fun in that?

Then there's the frog and cricket symphony that never allowed him to have a good night's sleep.

As far as Johnny was concerned, his father's regaling him with adventures and escapades from when he was Johnny's age sounded boring.

Nearly every house in Hardcastle Bridge had a name. Up Decker Cottage, Behind Bridge Manor, Whose House, Ha-Ha Palace, and so on. Johnny found the names hilarious.

Changing the neighborhood meant a change of school for Johnny. Not only was he having to adjust to starting at a new school, but he was also just starting high school.

Johnny's first day at school had been a disaster. The class teacher, Mrs. O'Brien, had asked something about the nine planets and Johnny had shot a hand up, eager to impress his new classmates.

"Mars—" he'd said.

"Mars" was all he said, not one word more.

But the entire class erupted with laughter until the teacher calmed them down. Johnny thought even Mrs. O'Brien had a small smile on her round face. He sat down that morning and never said a word in class after that. Not the day after, or the weeks to follow.

The local children of this Yorkshire village called him a snob because of his London accent. But their accent was weird too. He was struggling to fit in and often sat alone at lunch times.

He hated the quiet village, Hardcastle Craggs, and his new school. He just wanted to go back to where his home was. Back to London, among his friends.

CHAPTER THREE

Johnny Wheeler's Family – The Wheelers

Johnny's dad, John Neil, was a high-flying doctor whose exclusive practice just on the outskirts of the city had closed due to a fire and the death of a senior doctor. His mum, Sarah Jane, was a primary school English teacher.

The Wheelers had relocated to Hebden Bridge to join a family practice belonging to John's parents. John's dad was getting too old to keep up with the ever-increasing number of patients that came through the door.

The old man was forever thankful his son and his family were relocating to Hebden Bridge. Not just for the future of the practice, but for him and his equally aged wife to spend the next years having quality time with their son and his family.

Both John and Sarah were born and raised in the valley. They had even attended the same school as kids. After all, there isn't a lot of choice in a tiny village like Hebden Bridge.

Their paths didn't meet until the last year of high school when they ended up as partners at a school barn dance. John had two left feet and kept stepping on Sarah's feet, but they ended up laughing about it after John said sorry nearly every other step. Fate played its part, nearly every progressive dance inevitably found the two as partners.

When the pair left for different universities, they became pen pals and wrote endless letters to each other. During summer breaks, they both returned home and spent many summers in the woods at Hardcastle Craggs.

Unlike Johnny, returning to Hebden Bridge meant a return to home and peace for John and Sarah.

Their new home in Hardcastle Craggs, Cragg Cottage, was big and had space for a garden. They also didn't have a neighbour learning to play the piano at the expense of their eardrums, or a train honking a warning.

Cragg Cottage was nestled just off the main road down a small lane. About a half-hour's walk to the bus stop into Hebden Bridge for school or work.

The cottage was covered in red and gold ivy and had beautiful rose bushes lining the path. The rooms were spacious and filled with fresh, clean air.

Once again, Sarah fell in love with the cottage she recalled from her youth due to its quirky character.

CHAPTER FOUR

The Wheelers adopt a dog named Dog

One afternoon, the Wheelers visited the local animal shelter in Hebden Bridge. There, they adopted a small dog with a white fluffy coat and black round patches, from the local shelter. It was a Maltese and highland terrier mix, with floppy ears and a smiling face.

"Every boy should have a dog to go exploring with" Johnny's father had told him that afternoon.

Johnny fell in love with the dog immediately but had to tell his dad, this didn't mean he was happy to live here or bribed with the pet.

Neither Johnny nor his parents could agree on a name for the cute little fluff ball, so by default, his name ended up being Dog. It didn't help that the shelter hadn't given him a name. It was their policy not to get attached to pets, whether they were surrendered or found.

The Wheelers did try a few times to give the pooch a name. But no matter what they called him, he never responded or fetched the ball. In the end, they agreed to just call him Dog. They figured that it was the love they gave him that really mattered, not his name.

CHAPTER FIVE

Johnny visits the Wishing Well

Mornings at the Wheeler household were chaotic, with everyone rushing breakfast, getting their bags, and trying to get out on time. It was Johnny's job to make sure Dog had been out to the toilet, left enough food and water, and was locked in the yard so he wouldn't wander off.

After school, Johnny and Dog would venture out into the woods to explore till his mum rang the bell under the eaves to call him in for tea. This system worked wonderfully as it meant Johnny wasn't limited to staying within sight of the cottage.

There was an old wishing well just off the beaten path that most people never discovered.

The wooden roof was faded and warped; its stone walls needed repair. An old piece of rope hung from the cracked beam, but the bucket was long gone.

After another miserable day at school, Johnny ran into the woods and stumbled upon the old well.

Leaning over, he shouted "hello".

The sound echoed back "hello... hello," then faded gradually.

Johnny wondered how deep the well was, as he couldn't see the bottom. It was so deep and dark. He tossed in a penny and made a wish.

"I wish I could go back to London, "he let out a tired sigh, "or find a friend to play with".

Turning away, he ran back through the dappled wood to the cottage. He told his dad about the well, and John and Sarah shared an affectionate glance.

John turned to Johnny and said, "Ah, yes, the old well. It's magic you know," and ruffled his son's hair.

CHAPTER SIX

The Secret of the Wishing Well

Now, the well was home to a group of unlikely friends. They were an odd group, as you wouldn't normally think they had much in common, but maybe that is the glue that binds them together;

Tufty, a squirrel with a magnificent reddish tail and a tuft of reddish hair that flopped over his furry face, was definitely the leader of the group. He's a cheeky little fella, who was always up to mischief and provided his friends with many hilarious antics, full of crazy plans and ideas. Most of these plans didn't go according to how he planned, which made for never a dull moment.

Dottie, a petite and delicate brown doe, is more reserved and often tries to calm Tufty down when he comes up with the latest schemes. When things go pear-shaped, which they frequently do, she sighs but says nothing. Secretly she wishes she had more courage like her leader.

Freddie is the opposite of Dottie, and rather portly around the middle. Unlike most mice, Freddie is not averse to trying anything and everything new when he wants to eat. Dandelions are his absolute favorite food ever. He can get quite drunk on the weed, which he believes was all a mouse needed to live.

Dandelion tea, sandwiches, cakes, biscuits, soups.... there is nothing he can't make from it and sampling his wares gives him his "extra weight". Not that any of the gang would point that out, it just meant there was more of him to love.

Oscar, like all owls, is very wise and there isn't much that surprises him. His feathers are soft and brown which helps him blend in with the trees, so most people would miss seeing him if they weren't watching out for wildlife. He's very much respected by his fellow mates, but then has anyone ever heard of an unwise owl?

Candice was a stunning midnight black crow. Known to her friends as Candy, she's rather scatterbrained and the others often tease her by calling her Crazy Candy (they say insults are a form of flattery and Candy is very much loved so naturally gets lots of ribbing). However, if anyone outside of their group said any unkind word about the crow, the others would be quick to defend her. She was family and "no one messes with family" according to Tufty.

That night, deep in sleep, Johnny was woken by a constant tapping on the window. Half asleep, thinking it was the wind or trees, he opened the curtains and yelped as he came face to face with a furry animal with a magnificent reddish tail.

The animal was seemingly smiling.

"It must be a dream," Johnny thought.

He rubbed his eyes and opened them again, but it was still there.

Johnny cautiously opened the window a crack to shoo the animal away and then... it spoke.

"Hello Johnny, I'm Tufty. Want to come and play?"

Johnny scurried away from the window, only to have what was clearly a squirrel jump inside.

It brushed the flop of reddish hair covering its face backwards with a hand and sat on its hind legs. The animal's manners were more like a human's.

Johnny just stared and spluttered, "You talk...? Animals can't talk."

"Well, if you think I can't talk, why are you talking to me?" Tufty grinned. "The well heard your wish today and here I am, ready to be your friend and have lots of adventures. If you aren't too scared. The others are waiting for us at the well."

"Errm, I'm not scared," stated Johnny, standing up straight in his pj's. He peered out of the window. "Who are the others? How did you get up here?"

"Up the ivy of course," replied Tufty. "Let's go, time's wasting, and everyone is dying to meet you." He bounded back down to the ground and took off at a fast pace.

Johnny glanced out the window and saw the squirrel disappear into the woods.

"Did that squirrel just talk?" he muttered, staring into the dark bush ahead.

Despite the moonless night sky, he could still see the path where the squirrel had disappeared through.

"Must be a dream," he decided, before letting off a sleepy yawn.

The squirrel popped out of the woods and waved for Johnny to hurry. It disappeared into the woods after.

"It's not a dream?" he said, wide-eyed. "It's not a dream!"

Johnny made up his mind to follow. He slipped into a pair of joggers, never minding changing his pj's.

He gingerly climbed out onto the window ledge, turned round, and half climbed, half fell down the ivy. He had to run to keep up with the quick-footed Tufty, who was already out of sight.

Johnny wasn't sure how, but he could see clearly, which was baffling, having been used to London's streetlights, now there were a million small stars above him.

Hearing a noise behind him, he stopped and turned around to see Dog rushing up the path panting. To Johnny's amazement, Dog panted, "wait for me."

"Okay," Johnny said, absentmindedly. Then he froze as realization dawned on him. He turned around very slowly to face Dog. "No... wait... you can talk too... How come you never have before? Am I dreaming?"

"You hadn't ever wished before," Dog answered, breezing past Johnny. "But keep going or we won't get to join in the fun."

Johnny bobbed, smiling with excitement. He turned on his heels and bounded into the woods. Laughing as he ran.

Sometimes, he'd take the lead, other times it'd be Dog running after the quick-footed squirrel.

They reached the well and Johnny gasped yet again. Poised beside the well was a deer, and the fattest mouse he ever saw. And he'd seen a lot of mice in London.

A white-spotted brown owl perched on the rickety well roof, and a black crow on the edge of the well wall.

Tufty made the introductions and each in turn took a bow or flapped their wings.

Oscar's big eyes stared unblinking at the boy. "So glad to meet you, Johnny. It's going to be a fun night. Let's get going," he said, stretching his great wings.

Suddenly, the owl leapt into the air, somersaulted and dived into the well. The little crew of animals hopped up to the well, and jumped in one after the other.

Candy, just like Oscar, flew straight down into the dark hole. At last, it was just Johnny and Dog.

The canine tilted its head sideways. "You've gotta take a leap of faith, Johnny," he said as he jumped over the stone wall into the well with an excited holler.

Johnny looked into the dark depth and anxiously shouted, "Wait, I can't go in there. I can't swim". (There's not much call for swimming in London with its busy traffic and tall buildings.)

"It's ok, you don't need to swiiiiiimmmmmm," a falling voice echoed.

Johnny sat on the edge of the wall with his feet dangling in the empty space below. He was sweaty with worry and anxiety.

"What if I drown?" he thought aloud. "My mum will never forgive me... they won't ever find my body! I can't. I just can't."

Suddenly, a paw reached up and grabbed his foot, and pulled him into the well.

CHAPTER SEVEN

The beginning of an adventure

Johnny screamed and fell... in fact, he just kept falling and falling, into the water below and still falling.

After a mouth full of water, he clamped his lips tightly shut. "How can this be?" he thought. "It's so deep, it just keeps going but I'm not drowning. What's happening?"

Suddenly, Johnny landed on a softly padded piece of ground, surrounded by little coins and trinkets. His new friends stood around him, all smiling.

He laughed. "That was scary and fun all at the same time! How will I get back?"

"We told you it was ok, and don't worry about that," says Dottie the doe, smiling. "Let's go exploring, there's so much to see."

Colour flitted and turned everywhere Johnny looked. It was like watching a rainbow rise after a rainfall. Objects shimmered and glistened. It felt like the bottom of a vast ocean instead of the narrow bottom a well would supposedly have.

Johnny's eyes grew wider and wider the more he saw. All he could say was "Whoa! Wow! Cool!" laughter just bubbled out of him.

"So, what do you want to do?" asked Freddie, sitting on Dottie's back.

"I don't know," replied Johnny, still mesmerized by his surroundings.

"I know, let's go to the dam," chimed Tufty.

"No, wait. I can't go to the dam. I can't swim. And I'll get my pjs all wet. Mum won't like that," said Johnny, apprehensively.

"We can't go to the dam, Tufty, and you know why," came the deep voice of Oscar above Johnny's head.

"Why not?" asked Johnny.

Candy swooped down and sat on Johnny's shoulder. "Because," she said, "the water dragon doesn't let anyone near the water."

"Water dragon?"

"That's what I said," Candy insisted.

Johnny's eyes widened with excitement. "Wow! Is he big? What colour is he? Does he breathe fire? No, wait, no we can't go to see him. He will burn us all up. Nope, let's just go back. It's very late, I should be asleep. I could get into big trouble if mum comes to check on me and I'm nowhere to be found," said he.

"I'm with Johnny on this," squeaked Freddie the mouse.

"Oh, come on. How bad can it be? If we're quiet, he won't even know we are there," retorted Tufty and scurried off.

Dog ran after the squirrel, leaving Johnny no choice but to follow. He couldn't bear the thought of the dragon eating his dog, his dad would ground him for life.

"Fine," he said, sighing as he ran after them. "Just don't wake the dragon!"

CHAPTER EIGHT

The water dragon is awakened

The merry band of seven reached the section of the river they needed to cross to get to the dam. On the other side was a sign that read, "Private property, keep out."

Tufty leapt over to the first round rock in the water and continued to hop left and right, finding stones to land on till he reached the other side.

"Come on," he yelled, covering his mouth with his small hands.

"Oh well, let's go," said Dottie, and stepped into the icy water. It was so cold her whole body shivered, and Freddie nearly fell from her back. He grabbed on tight with both feet and just hoped she didn't slip. Though a good swimmer, Freddy didn't fancy a splash in the dark waters!

"You'll have to carry me, Johnny," said Dog. "My legs are too short to jump the rocks, and the water is too fast. It will wash me downstream."

So, Johnny scooped Dog into his arms like a newborn and held him to his chest. He looked at the flowing river before him. It was probably as wide as his grandpa's truck.

Thinking to himself, "it might wash me away," he cautiously took the first little jump. With each step getting him closer to the other side, he became quite excited.

"Look at me," he laughed, taking the last jump.

However, he didn't land correctly and started to wobble and slip on the wet surface. Just when he thought he was going to fall into the river, Oscar and Candy each grabbed one of his shoulders and half dragged, half flew him to the grassy ground. They all lay about laughing.

Tufty got up first. "Come on, let's climb up to the dam," he said and dashed off. Johnny looked at the others. They were looking back at him.

"He always gets us into trouble," Freddie said, trying to fight his way through the long tall grass.

"He just likes adventure," said Dottie.

"Hmm," was all Oscar replied.

Johnny picked up Freddie and put him in his pocket.

"It's okay, I'll carry you, Freddie," he said, taking off after the squirrel. After all, he was very curious to see if the water dragon was real.

Everyone fell in line and approached the dam steps.

"Shh, quiet," whispered Dottie as she struggled up the uneven stone steps. (Deer are not mountain goats, she thought). "We don't want to wake the dragon."

They all got to the top and just stared.

"Wow, does it go on forever?" Johnny whispered.

From his pocket, Freddie took a gulp. This was an ocean, not a dam. (Field mice naturally have a very small view of life).

The crow and owl sat on a tree branch overhanging the water. It was so deep, it looked like a great big pit. Not very inviting at all.

"What are you *doing* Tufty?" whispered Dottie. The others turned just in time to see Tufty do a swan dive into the water.

He surfaced and laughed. "Come on in, the water isn't cold," splashing and showing off his acrobatic skills.

"I thought he said we wouldn't wake the dragon," Johnny asked Oscar the owl.

"Tufty's plans always go the worst possible way," said Oscar.

"What?" Tufty the squirrel screamed in the same dam he'd said a dragon lived. "Yay! So much fun," he squalled in the same dam he said they'll be quiet at.

When he looked at their faces, all were staring, not at him, but at something behind him. He slowly turned round and came face to face with fiery yellow eyes, wide nostrils blasting white smoke into the night air, and bared giant teeth.

It was an angry face, this much he could tell without a doubt. Whilst deciding what best to do, swim or stay still, the dragon opened his mouth and drew in a gulp of air. A ball of fire ignited in the dragon's throat.

Everyone drew a horrified gasp.

The dragon was going to blow back a stream of fire!

CHAPTER NINE

How to beat a dragon without a fight

"**W**AIT!"

All eyes, including the dragon, turned and looked at Johnny, who was now wishing he had kept his mouth shut tight. He swallowed.

"We didn't mean any harm, Mr. Dragon. We were just admiring your beautiful dam and how vast the water is."

The dragon turned back towards the center and lifted two mighty wings from the water and took off. All eyes were glued on him. He was so big the only thing Johnny could think of was that he was bigger than the biggest of buildings in London. He also realized that they were in trouble because the dragon looked very angry.

The dragon looked like a snake with smooth midnight-blue fur. Its wings stretched from end to end like those of those great planes flying over London. It had four legs, and two pairs of short goat horns.

Tufty still hadn't moved. He was also just staring at the giant monster, who was a lot bigger than he'd imagined.

"I'm never going to do something stupid like this again, ever," he thought if indeed he wasn't going to be burnt to a crisp or eaten tonight.

The mighty dragon swooped and his wings made a huge flapping sound. The wind they created knocked most of the group to the floor. Even the two birds were blown out of the tree they perched on.

Tufty had swum back to the edge and was being blown out of the water with the wind. His tuft of fur fell over his eyes.

It was then that he noticed the side of the dragon.

Water dragons, unlike other dragons, don't have scales. It seemed more fur-like than anything else. Sticking out of the dragon's side was a spiked metal bar.

Just as the dragon opened his enormous mouth to breathe his fire, Tufty shouted, "Stop, please Mr. Dragon! We can help you. You poor thing, it must be painful with that spike in your side. If you don't eat us or burn us, we can help you get it out."

"What are you doing?" Dottie whispered.

"He's hurt," said Tufty. "We have to help him."

"*We?*" squeaked Freddie. "Have you seen how big he is and how small we are? I wouldn't even be an entire bite."

The call had stilled the dragon, who was now just flapping his great wings above the water, and stared at the group. His eyes held pain and sorrow, even though his mouth looked grim and angry.

Johnny took a deep breath and stood on the edge of the water.

"Hello dragon," he said in a trembling voice. "We didn't mean any harm, we just wanted to swim in the beautiful water. If we help you remove the bar from your side, maybe you could let us go and not eat us?"

"I don't know if he understands what I said," Johnny told the others. "Maybe he comes from another country and doesn't speak the same language as us. My dad had patients who didn't understand him or couldn't speak at all. But my dad always helped them, and that's the right thing to do with him too."

"Very wise," hooted Oscar the owl.

The dragon took off in full flap and circled above them, then came to land on the grassy bank. Motionless, he waited. So did the others. No one was too keen to move or speak.

Dottie, being the big-hearted, soft deer she was, approached the dragon slowly. When she reached his giant head, she gently rubbed her neck against his throat. She could feel the heat of the fire inside but stood fast.

Candy flew towards the bar and took in the situation. It was quite deep and she wasn't sure they had the strength to pull It out. After all, what can two birds, a mouse, and a deer do? They had no hands. If anyone was going to help the dragon, it would have to be Tufty and Johnny. Both of whom seemed to reach the same conclusion at the same time as her.

"You have to help him," she crowed. "The poor thing must be in so much pain."

Johnny approached the dragon and started cooing, just like he had seen his dad do with patients. Just soft little noises made to soothe the fear. The dragon stood waiting, watching with those huge yellow eyes. Johnny held out his arm, and with a big gulp, touched the dragon, all the while still cooing as best as he could being so fearful himself.

The dragon's body shuddered and for one dreadful moment Johnny thought " he's gonna eat me" ...another breath, and he gave a huge sigh... so far so good.

Johnny and Tufty went to the dragon's side and stared at the bar that was stuck in its side. It was just below his wing and way too high for either of them to reach. The bar looked like a long spear with sharp nails all over it.

"What shall we do? I'm too little, I can't reach," said Johnny.

Oscar had been studying the situation for a while and being wise, knew they would need some extraordinary plan if this was to succeed. Plus, if they didn't succeed, none of them would be going home, this he was sure of. Oscar shuddered at the thought of becoming dragon's toast. He began barking out orders.

"Tufty, climb up that tree and along the branch so it bends down towards the dragon. Dottie, stand next to the dragon's side as close as you can. Johnny, climb up onto Dottie and then up on the wing," he said.

"No, it's too high to climb and poor Dottie isn't big so you'll hurt her," said Freddie.

Candy glanced over to Oscar and nodded her beak in agreement. "It's the only way," she said.

Tufty looked at the dragon, then at the tree and he too started nodding. This was getting to be exciting.

Poor Johnny was still not keeping up with the plan and looked very confused.

Speaking to the dragon Oscar said. "I don't know if you understand me, but here's what we are going to do. Tufty will climb the tree and go along the branch right to the end so it bends down. Johnny will climb up Dottie's back and then onto your wing. We will fasten the branch to the bar and then Tufty will jump down, and the branch will swing back up and take the bar with it. Simple."

"That's all well and good", Candy trilled. "But what are you going to fasten the branch to the bar with?"

Everyone just looked around at each other. They hadn't thought of that!

Suddenly, Dog spoke up. "My collar," he said. "Take it off and fasten the bar to the branch with that."

"Excellent idea Dog. I was just about to say that," hooted Oscar, his round eyes unblinking. It seemed to Johnny that Oscar was "always going to say that" after someone else had spoken the words.

Johnny took the collar off, looked back at the dragon, and said, "Here goes nothing."

Poor Dottie, her spindly legs were shaking as Johnny climbed on her back and her knees started to buckle. Johnny started to wobble and couldn't find anything to hold onto. Just when the whole thing looked like it would fail, the dragon turned his neck towards his wing. He groaned as the bar moved in his side. Johnny ended up between the dragon's neck and Dottie's back, safe from falling. He took a moment to breathe and scrambled up till he sat on the wing. It looked a long way down and he gulped.

Dog, meanwhile, was jumping around wagging his fluffy tail and shouting, "you've got this Johnny, look at you"

"That's not really helping," stated Freddie, who felt totally useless to help in any way.

Tufty was sitting in the tree, eagerly waiting for some action. He tried to edge closer and closer to the tiny tip and his weight bowed the branch down, but just not enough to reach the side of the dragon.

Flying around everyone, giving orders as he went, Oscar organized the whole rescue perfectly. Candy flew upon the branch next to Tufty to add her weight and little Freddie scurried up the tree, after all, he had considerable weight he could add too, he might only be small, but it had to help.

It worked wonderfully, the branch was close enough for Johnny to tie the collar around it and the bar.

"Right, after three when I say jump, everyone off the branch," shouted Oscar.

"One, two, three, jump!"

What a sight it would have been to see. The branch snapped back upright and the bar moved. The poor dragon opened his giant mouth and the flames shot out high and far like a fiery comet. It was a terrible sound to hear and all jumped back not knowing what had happened. Johnny, still on the dragon's back, dared not move at all.

They turned to look. The bar wasn't completely out, the tip still inside the dragon's side. They had failed.

No one spoke.

All eyes turned to the dragon...was this it? Would they now get burned or eaten by making him even angrier? Freddie went and hid in Dottie's fur, peering out fearfully. Dog had stopped barking and Tufty and Candy who had recovered from their jump were also just standing very still.

Johnny looked at the giant dragon's eyes and tears filled his. He had thought he would be able to help, just like his dad did with his patients. Now things were worse.

"Right, everyone, gather round," said Oscar. "We are going to have round two...places everyone."

No one moved, all still staring at the dragon not knowing what was to come.

The dragons 'eyes started to fill with water and his tears slid down his face. His breath was ragged and short, puffs of smoke coming from his nostrils.

He took one more breath and turned his neck again towards his wing where Johnny was still sitting.

"It's ok, my friend. We will get you fixed," Johnny whispered in that soothing voice again. He just knew that his dad would not give up on an injured person, and neither would he.

Everyone seemed to understand without words what to do next, and all got into place. The difference this time was Freddie. The dog's collar was still at the tip of the bar which was no good. It needed to be further down towards the wing to have any effect. Freddie was the lightest so he ran up the bar and pushed with all his might at the collar, (his extra belly weight was coming in handy) which ever so slowly moved down. It seemed to take forever, and Tufty was getting impatient. Candy poked him with her beak. He got the message after a quick ouch.

"On the count of three everyone. One, two, three...jump," Oscar shouted.

The tree branch twanged and flew up...Tufty not quick enough on the jump went flying into the air.

Instead of being scared, he shouted loudly... "look at me, I'm a flying squirrel!"

The bar came out and clanged to the floor. Everyone cheered and danced. They all turned to look at the dragon. Now I'm not sure dragons can smile, but it seemed to Johnny that's exactly what was happening. He slid down the side of the dragon and along with his friends stood in front of his huge face. A face which no longer looked angry and frightening, but calmed. The tears had stopped and the mighty giant bent down his head and bowed to the small group.

"Thank you!" the dragon said.

CHAPTER TEN

The Dragon's story

They all quickly looked up in awe at the beautiful sound that came from the dragon's lips. The words sounded like a melody. Not what they expected from the giant. Plus, he could talk.

They all started talking at once, both to each other and the dragon.

He raised his mighty head and spoke.

"My name is George; I am the last of the water dragons and I am in your service for a debt I cannot repay. Ages have come and gone whilst I have been earthbound with the spear named Destroyer. Long ago they hunted me for my magic. Dragons' tears heal even the worst of ailments and give long life if not immortality. They captured me and tried in vain to make me shed tears for their gain. But I said I would rather die than give them my gift. They told me death was too good for me, so impaled me with the spear and I fell here into the dam where I lost my voice, silenced by pain.

"I made my home at the bottom of the dam fearful that man would discover me and use me. The last owner closed the dam and I could live undisturbed. Now I think man has forgotten about me. It could be safe to soar once more.

"I am sorry if I frightened you, I have lived so long in a silent world without companions. I would be honored to call you friends if you would accept me."

Everyone started talking at once. Questions sprang from everyone's lips and their excitement was hardly containable.

To have a dragon for a friend? How pleasant that would be!

"Jump aboard my back and I will soar in the night sky and show you my strength."

Everyone jumped or scrambled up, Johnny carrying Dog and pulling poor Dottie up by her hooves...very undignified, but she wasn't complaining. Oscar and Candy waited to fly alongside. George chuckled and shouted "keep up if you can!" and sprung into the air.

His majestic wings stretched out and his immense body floated like a feather on the breeze. Candy and Oscar quickly realized they were no match for their new found-friend so perched on a branch nearby and waited. What a magical sight. The huge midnight blue body glistened in the light, and a silver streak along his forehead shone.

Round and round the dam they flew, diving down only to soar back up. The wind in their faces with the stars surrounding them, magic filled the air.

After some time, George landed on the grass at the bottom of the dam and all scrambled off. The air was filled with laughter and joy, something George had not heard for too long. He let out a sigh and closed his eyes.

Johnny did the same thing. He was starting to get tired from all the adventure and was sure it should have been morning by now. He was too tired to worry about what his parents would say when he got home. He was even too tired to worry about how he would get home.

He stretched on the grass, determined to rest only a few minutes and leave for home. Within moments he was fast asleep.

"Johnny, wake up. You've slept in," called his mother.

He shot up straight and looked around. "Huh? How did I get home?" He glanced at the mat next to the bed and saw Dog sound asleep.

"Dog, Dog, wake up, it's morning and we're home." Dog lifted his head, looked at Johnny, and went back to sleep.

Johnny raced downstairs, flew into the kitchen, and started babbling about wells, animals and dragons. His dad just looked at him with a twinkle in his eye and gently said, "Dreams are wonderful adventures, aren't they?"

Johnny just knew it wasn't a dream and he couldn't wait for bedtime to come around again. He finally had friends, even if no one believed him.

Friends who he could have so many adventures with. Life in Hebden Bridge finally started to look good to the little boy. He was so glad they had moved.

BOOK TWO

CHAPTER ELEVEN

Johnny's friends disappear

A few weeks after starting school, Johnny was still struggling in the friend department. It seemed if you weren't born in Yorkshire, you would never be accepted. They called him a snob, but as far as he was concerned, it was they who had the problem speaking. He couldn't understand most of what they said in their funny accent.

John and Jenny had noticed how quiet Johnny was concerning talking about school and friends. They kept attempting to unsuccessfully convince each other that it just takes time. Silently, they were both starting to get a bit worried about their son.

When Johnny started having a bit more positivity about him, this confirmed to his parents he'd finally made friends much to their relief. Once or twice one of his parents would suggest Johnny have a friend over after school, to which Johnny would make some excuse as to why not. What his parents didn't realize was the friends he had made were not people. They had no idea Johnny had found magical friends in the wishing well!

Johnny was often distracted doing his homework, His mum was constantly checking up on him.

He'd rush through it and as soon as finished, would call the dog and disappear into the woods.

At first, after his night-time adventure, Johnny thought he'd see his friends whenever he went to the well. But, after waiting for what seemed an eternity and endless calling of names, the disheartened boy would go home. When he went to bed, he would try his hardest not to fall asleep hoping to hear a tap on his window. Soon he began to think the whole adventure must have only been a dream after all. Even the dog didn't look or act any different.

Eventually, he gave up going to the well and would go and explore different trails. Once or twice, he would wander down to the river where they had crossed to the dam and look hopefully across, only to be disappointed.

Then one night when he had given up hope, he was woken by a persistent tapping. He sat up straight in the bed thinking he must have misheard the noise. But no, there it was again.

He rushed to the window and pulled back the curtains to see Tufty sitting on the ledge. He flung the window open, nearly knocking the poor squirrel over, grabbed him with two hands and hugged him tight.

Questions tumbled out, "where had he been, where were the others, why hadn't they come back, why couldn't he see them?" He garbled "I've missed you so much"

"Whoa whoa", said Tufty. "You're talking so fast I can't understand you. And I'm a squirrel."

Johnny blushed painfully. "Sorry," he said, still brimming with excitement.

Tufty waved a small hand. "Come with me, and bring some chalk, we're off to the well to meet the others."

Then he was gone.

CHAPTER TWELVE

There's no danger in Tufty's plan

Johnny looked back over his shoulder to see Dog sitting there and watching him. He shook his head, grabbed some chalk and climbed out the window and down the ivy to the ground. He ran as fast as his little legs would carry him straight to the well. Glancing to the side, he saw Dog keeping pace with him. He got to the clearing and stopped. Sitting there were the five friends.

Everyone started talking at the same time, and then they all started laughing.

"I've missed you so much," Johnny said, laughing." Where have you been? Every day I've looked for you."

Owl spoke, "Time is different for us. It's only been one day since we were at the dam."

"Gosh it feels like forever to me," Johnny said. "I thought I would never see you again. I'm just so glad to see you all. Can we go down the well again and have an adventure?"

"Tufty has another *idea,*" Candy said, ominously.

"I promise you, there's zero danger with this one," said Tufty, clasping his small hands.

Dottie smiled. "Come on, Johnny. Let's show you."

Everyone set off and Johnny and the dog fell in line. He chatted the whole way, so excited to finally know he hadn't dreamt of them and he was going to have another adventure.

After winding through the woods, the track came to the river. Not, like Johnny had thought, to the dam, but much further. They stopped just short of the waterwheel, at the stepping stones.

"Come on," said Tufty, and they all jumped the steps over to the other side. It all looked so magical in the moonlight with a million diamonds in the sky.

Once on the other side, they marched in single file towards the big boulder. "Chalk please". Johnny dug into PJ's pockets and produced a small stick. Tufty outlined a door on the rock and stood back.

Nothing happened.

He drew over the outline again, but still nothing.

Oscar flew down to the ground and looked up. "Silly squirrel, you haven't drawn a doorknob," he hooted.

"Whoops, forgot," smiled Tufty and proceeded to rectify that.

"What's gonna hap... Whoa, can you see that?" Johnny's excited voice proclaimed. "It's a door".

Sure, enough the outline of the door was glowing bright white light.

"Oh, do be careful," whispered Dottie. "You never know what's on the other side."

Freddie, munching on a dandelion, watched as Tufty opened the door and stepped through.

Everyone waited, but he didn't come back out.

"I told you," said Dottie, "now what's he got himself into?"

"It's ok Dottie, I'll go check on him," Johnny said, as he took a step towards the door.

"No, wait, let me fly through and see what's on the other side before anyone else goes missing."

"Don't you know where he's gone?" asked Johnny.

Turning her delicate face towards him, Dottie quietly said, "It's a magic door that leads to places unknown. Whenever you step through the door it takes you to a different place every time. If we all step through it separately, we could all end up in different places."

"We need to all go together," said Candy the crow.

"Good point," said Oscar, who now took it upon himself to take charge yet again. "Let's count to three and all step through together. One. Two. Three!"

Everyone stepped through the door. There was a rush of air and a light so bright you couldn't see anything for the glare. There was a loud thwack as they all fell into a long and narrow boat known as a kayak.

Even more, the kayak was rocking violently on a wide raging river.

No sooner were they in the kayak, it left the bank and started going very fast with the current. Candy and Oscar, who were both sitting on Dottie's back, flew into the air.

Johnny sat up and looked about to try to find an oar or something with which to steer the boat. There was nothing. Holding onto the edges he started to panic.

Once again, he was in the middle of the water, not being able to swim. He really needed to ask his parents for swimming lessons at this rate. Poor Dottie wasn't faring much better. Sitting in the bottom of the kayak wide-eyed and shaking. There was no sign of Tufty.

"I'm going to scout ahead to see where we are going and if Tufty is close by," said Oscar.

He flew up into the night sky. After what seemed like forever, he flew back to the others.

"I've found Tuffy" he hooted. "It's not good. His boat has crashed into some rocks in the middle of the river further down. It's smashed up and he has climbed up onto the rocks. We're going to have to rescue him."

Dog, who had been quiet until now, spoke up, "And how do we rescue him when we need rescuing ourselves? In case it slipped your notice, we have nothing to steer with. We may end up smashed on the same rocks!"

"I have an idea," crowed Candy. "What if we all went to one side and that would make the boat go in that direction? We can come alongside Tufty and he can jump in."

"Your crazy Candy," retorted Oscar.

The poor raven looked so downcast; Johnny felt sorry for her. Trying his best to sound confident he spoke. "That sounds like a very good plan Candy and I think we should try it. Come on everyone, over to the left side."

To everyone's surprise, the boat started to veer to the left.

"I'm sorry Candy," Oscar said, apologizing. "I wasn't trying to be mean to you, you're my friend and friends don't do that. Well done. I will fly down to Tufty and tell him the plan. He can't be that far away now".

Oscar came back a few moments later. "Tufty is just up ahead. I told him the plan and he'll be ready to jump. Everyone over to the right side."

The rocking boat slowly started to go towards the middle of the river. They could see Tufty just ahead waving his paws.

"Why did I listen to the squirrel," Johnny thought. "He might tip the kayak over jumping in and we'll all drown."

Dottie was right. Tufty's ideas never went well. The kayak was heading straight for the rocks, if they weren't careful, they'd crash too.

"Switch to the left now," yelled Oscar, trying to be heard above the noise of the rushing water.

They did and the boat straightened, fairly close to the rocks.

"You're gonna have to jump as we pass," Johnny yelled to the squirrel. Tufty stood up and launched himself off the rocks towards the boat.

Johnny leaned towards the squirrel with both hands stretched out. There was a loud thud as the squirrel hit the side of the kayak. He was half in and half out of the vessel and Johnny was pulling with all his might to get him in.

Drenched and looking rather like a drowned rat, Tufty lay with his eyes closed. There was a smile on his face. He opened his eyes and jumped to his feet.

"Woo hoo! Did you see that magnificent jump? That was so much fun."

Looking around, Tufty saw there were twelve sets of eyes glaring at him. He swallowed and chuckled nervously.

"Oh, come on everyone, we're fine. Lighten up and enjoy yourselves. Where's your sense of adventure?"

Suddenly Freddie yelled, "Erm, I don't want to spoil your fun Tufty, but look ahead everyone, the water disappears."

No one spoke.

The fast-moving water was disappearing into the air. Could water suddenly disappear into thin air?

Of course not!

They were heading straight towards a waterfall. Candy and Oscar would be fine, but the others- well it didn't look at all good for them.

Everyone in the kayak started screaming at once, paddling backwards with small paws and thin hooves.

"What do we do," yelled Johnny over the noise.

"Keep calm," Oscar yelled back.

"Keep calm?! How can we keep calm when we're all going to die." Freddie squealed.

Once again, Oscar's wisdom stopped the full-on panic.

"Ok, Freddie," he said, "get into Johnny's pocket. Dottie, Lie on the floor. Johnny grabs Dog's collar and lays over Dottie. Wedge your feet against the sides of the kayak. Tufty, lie between dog and Johnny and hold hands. Both of you keep a hand on the side of the boat and everyone hangs on tight. Please everyone, hurry."

Somehow, despite the ensuing madness, everyone did as told, just in time for their fall.

The kayak flew over the edge and hung in mid-air for a split second. Then it fell forward and flew straight down like an arrow.

Everyone screamed.

CHAPTER THIRTEEN

The silver-haired sisters

Oscar and Candy lost sight of their friends in the thunderous waters and they couldn't get any closer or they'd get caught in the waters themselves.

Johnny had hold of the boat so tight he felt his hand would snap. Head down, water smashing over the top of him, he lost all sense of time. Down, down, down. Going faster and faster, the boat plummeted.

Smack!

They hit the water and the momentum kept them vertical as it went under so they looked like a diving submarine. That is if submarines didn't have roofs.

In all the turmoil everyone got tossed out.

Johnny had no idea what was happening to everyone. It was dark, the water tossing him over and over. He stopped fighting and surrendered to the inevitable.

He felt someone grab his ankle and feared it was an octopus. But instead of pulling him down as an octopus would, it was pulling him up.

His head surfaced and he was dragged ashore. He fell onto the bank still gasping. Johnny lay there and closed his eyes, heart pounding in his chest. Ever so slowly his heart slowed and reason returned.

Johnny opened his eyes and blinked. Sitting next to him in the moonlight was an amazing sight. There was a girl smiling at him. It took a moment to register that it was a girl, as all he could see was silver hair floating down to her waist with the bluest eyes he had ever seen.

Totally captivated, Johnny was feeling very foolish. He tried to speak, whilst at the same time turning to look for his friends.

"My friends, where are my friends?" he asked, searching the river surface. "We have to help them."

"It's ok Johnny, they are all here, take a look.

Again, he turned and looked at the girl. Her voice sounded like tinkling bells, holding him in a trance.

He blushed. "Sorry, it's rude to stare, but who are you?"

She didn't reply but got up and walked over to a group of a soggy-looking bunch of animals. Johnny ran over and threw his arms around his friends and hugged them so tight, they started protesting.

"We're all fine Johnny, look and see," whispered Dottie.

Sure enough, not only were they all fine but Freddie was eating a dandelion.

Trying to think, as much as a twelve-year-old can after nearly drowning, he turned once again to the girl.

She, along with three identical other girls all with silver flowing hair and diamond eyes, was smiling at him. A million questions tumbled out of his mouth so fast, he had to stop to catch his breath.

"Let me explain," the girls said, laughing. "My name is Essie and these are my sisters, Esther, Esmai and Ellie. We are nymphs, this is our home. We knew you were coming over the falls, the fish told us. We don't get many visitors and when we do, it's not usually from the kingdom above. We live in the river and play under the falls. So, we waited here to catch you and keep you safe."

Johnny looked over at his friends and sure enough, there was Tufty ginning like a Cheshire cat, whilst squeezing water out of his tail.

"Wasn't that great?" he exclaimed, excitedly. "Such an adventure! We should do it again sometime."

"NO!" everyone chorused at once.

Tufty blinked, surprised.

"Tufty, every time we do things you suggest we end up in trouble. Johnny can't swim and along with us could have drowned," said Dottie.

"No one has ever died coming over the falls," said Essie, with twinkling eyes and her smile lighting up her face. "Why don't we all go to our house and have refreshments before you go home?"

"Do you have dandelions?" you-know-who asked.

"Yes," Essie said, chuckling. "Lots of them."

"Well, I'm in then, I'm starving. What about you Dog?"

"I am too," he barked.

Johnny, still captivated by the silver hair and lilting voice, stood up and nodded.

Not so far down the path they came to a clearing with enormous mushrooms in the middle. Why? One of the mushrooms was as big as a circus tent.

Essie went straight over to the biggest and to everyone's surprise a door appeared.

They all stepped in and stared. Inside the mushroom was a large room filled with shiny objects scattered around. There were little mushroom stools and a table made from wood in the center, full of food.

Johnny looked carefully around.

Upon closer inspection, Johnny realized the shiny objects scattered around were bracelets and rings lost by people and found by the nymphs. A veritable treasure trove.

Secondly, he noticed the food. It was not human food, but flowers and green stalks mixed with berries and nuts.

Essie smiled at him and said, "Please, help yourself. The flowers are a variety of flavors, so try one."

"I'm sorry, I don't really eat flowers," Johnny said.

"Ah, but these are special, they taste like your favorite food."

Everyone else was tucking into the various foods, munching away merrily and exclaiming how wonderful they taste.

Johnny picked up a yellow flower and bit into it. He immediately stopped chewing and gasped.

"It tastes like banana flavored bubble-gum," he declared, stuffing more into his mouth.

He soon discovered everyone had a different taste, which all agreed did indeed taste like their favorite food.

They sat around on the stools and listened to the nymphs tell stories. As much as he wanted to listen to all the adventures, Johnny started to feel very tired and yawned several times.

"I really think I need to go home, I'm very tired after all the excitement and danger. It must be morning by now. How do I get home? If I don't get up for school my parents will worry, and I am so tired I don't think I could even wake up to go," he said, followed by yet another yawn.

"That's all taken care of by my friends, so no need to worry. I have a friend of yours coming here to take you home." She looked out of the window and turned back to the group. "Your ride is here, come on everyone."

Going back through the door, everyone looked and gave an excited cry.

"George! How wonderful to see you again."

The dragon was sitting on the ground, smiling at them. "I've been on lots of adventures of my own," he said in his sing-songy voice. "It's been wonderful to fly once more and there are so many new and exciting places to visit. But, come along now, everyone hops up and I'll take you back to Hardcastle Craggs."

They all got on George's back and waved goodbye to the sisters.

"Come again to see us," the sisters called. With a huge rush of air, George took off and flew in spirals up the waterfall. A few moments later he landed in the clearing where the wishing well was.

All jumped down and thanked their friend.

"Come on Johnny," said Dog, "back to the house. Bye, everyone, thank you for a very big adventure."

"Wait for me dog," shouted Johnny.

He turned, smiled at his friends and ran off after his dog. He glanced back once, but the clearing was empty. He climbed the ivy and fell into the room. He went to his bed and lay on it and immediately fell asleep. Next to the bed on his rug, Dog was also sound asleep.

CHAPTER FOURTEEN

Magic isn't magic in real time

When his mum called him down for breakfast Johnny jumped out of bed. He started getting out of his pj"s and noticed a flower still in his pocket.

"Hmm I wonder what flavour this is," he thought and took a bite. He spat it straight back out. It tasted like one time he ate an ant in his oats.

"Gross," he muttered. Clearly magic flowers were not magic in real-time.

Dog just looked at him and said nothing.

"Ah, well," Johnny laughed. "Come one Dog, it's breakfast time."

When he entered the kitchen smiling, his mum asked him why. "Oh, I've just been on a big adventure mum. I nearly drowned and everything."

He sat and started eating his coco pops.

"Ah, yes, Johnny, I remember all the stories your dad told me, of dreams about adventures he had when he was your age living here. It's so lovely to see you have the same wonderful imagination.

Hurry up now or you'll be late for the bus."

Johnny just shrugged his shoulders and finished his cereal.

BOOK THREE

CHAPTER FIFTEEN

The freezing season

Winter was coming and the trees had all shed their leaves and the woods looked very bleak indeed. The winter nights rolled around quickly and made long walks impossible.

Johnny had been out to play a few times in his wellies, all togged up.

The tourists had all gone and the only people to see were the locals taking a walk. It was very muddy underfoot and several times his mother had reprimanded him for leaving the dirty wellies in the kitchen instead of in the outhouse used as a laundry.

Once or twice he had met up with his woodland friends at the well, but there had been no adventures. Even the animals felt the chill in the air and wanted to stay inside where it was warm.

November rolled into December and the snow came. Now snow is wonderful to play in and make snowmen, but Johnny found no pleasure trudging through knee-deep snow every day to the bus stop. If this kept up he would soon be able to stay at home.

The valley, you see, has zones, depending on where you live. If you lived in zone D you lived at the bottom of the valley and never got to have time off school for being snowed in as the snow plough kept the roads clear. The higher up you lived, the heavier it snowed and settled.

High on the tops was zone A. Most school children who lived up there loved winter. Once the buses couldn't get up due to the snow, it was an unscheduled holiday. Johnny lived in zone B and was seriously hoping the snow would be deep enough for his zone to be impacted.

That day came and Johnny was super excited. His poor parents had to battle the weather to get down into the village. Doctors did not take time off just because it snowed. It was suggested that Johnny accompany his dad to the surgery, but after a lot of complaining and begging, they relented.

"Just don't go too far into the woods if you play out" his mother shouted out, getting into the four-wheel drive.

Johnny's only thought was staying out of the cold and watching cartoons. He did have schoolwork to do, but he would leave it as long as possible.

He was so engrossed in the cartoon he was watching; it took a while for him to realize he could hear some knocking. He ran up to his bedroom and looked out the window. Tufty was sitting there madly tapping, looking very cold. Johnny was very curious as he had never seen his friends during the day, it was always at night.

He went to the window and opened it, to have Tufty jump straight in.

"Hello Tufty, this is a nice surprise."

"We need your help urgently. Dottie has been kidnapped by an ice troll!

You have to come straight away."

CHAPTER SIXTEEN

To the land of ice

"What is an ice troll, it sounds very scary?"

"There are three kinds of trolls. The most dangerous are cave trolls. They eat and kill any and everything. Lucky for us, there aren't any living near us. Then there are rock trolls. Most of the time they keep to themselves. Baby rock trolls are fun to play with. Rock trolls move around a lot so it's hard to make friends with them. They are scared of the cave trolls due to being twice the size of an adult rock troll.

"Then there are the ice trolls. We only ever see them in winter and they usually stick to the hills. There are a few who are nice and others who...well...can be very bad-tempered. The one who took Dottie is the latter. A bad ice troll. We are really worried about Dottie in case they eat her...deer are a delicacy to all trolls."

Johnny shuddered at the thought of losing one of his wonderful friends.

"What do we do? How can we save her if they are bigger than us?" he asked, panicking.

"Oscar has a plan, but only he can explain it. Come on, no time to waste."

Tufty jumped up onto the ledge and out the window before Johnny could count to three. He ran down the stairs and grabbed his kagoole, gloves, scarf and his wellies.

He called Dog who was sitting by the fire, curled into a ball. "Our friends need our help dog, let's go."

The wind was blowing hard and took his breath away for a moment. He ran as fast as he could in the deep snow and ice, to the well where the others were waiting impatiently.

Trying to catch his breath, he panted out. "What's the plan?"

Oscar the owl spoke up. "Right," he began, clearing his throat. "We are going down the well. The boulder door would be quicker, but it's not a guarantee it will take us where we want to go and we can't waste any time."

Once that was decided, everyone took a turn hopping up and into the well.

Johnny had forgotten how deep the well was and once in the water, he remembered to keep his mouth closed. He was expecting to land on the soft grass as before, but it was a very bumpy landing on rocks. He grazed his knee and came to a sudden stop.

"Ouch," he winced.

This was a very different landscape. Upon inspection he noticed they were on the top of a small hill in the middle of nowhere and just ahead was a stone-pointed shaped weird building he had never seen before.

The area around was littered with boulders and rocks protruding out of the frozen ground. Everything else was covered under layers of thick snow. The air was rather foggy and very, very cold. Colder, if possible than the woods.

Johnny pulled his hat further down and turned to the others. "Where are we?"

Tufty stepped up to answer. "This place is called Stoodley Pike. It's a monument from an old battle. In summer, it is very popular with tourists who walk up from Hebden Bridge. The rock trolls take refuge here and in summer we come and play a game with them; rock throwing."

"Really?" asked Johnny, who was now itching to see what a troll looked like.

"There is a young rock troll called Ricky," Tufty continued. "We never win of course, but it's fun anyway. We climb to the top of the pike with the steps inside, to the top and hurl rocks as hard as we can. Let's go see if we can find him and maybe he can tell us where Dottie is."

CHAPTER SEVENTEEN

A rock troll joins the army

The small group set off at a brisk pace, crunching on icy grass and stepping in big frozen mud puddles that were everywhere. The nearer they got to the pike the bigger it looked to Johnny. He could see what looked like a balcony halfway up. They got to the opening and Tufty went in first. Oscar and Candy would fly up and meet them at the top.

Johnny didn't realize, as no one told him, but it was pitch black going up the steps. It was a case of putting one foot in front of the other and hoping for the best. Something furry ran past his legs.

"Ahh what's that...there's something in here. Tufty, where are you?"

"Don't panic Johnny, it's only a sheep. They wander up and down here all the time," Freddie squeaked.

Johnny's heart slowed back to normal. He sighed. He could see a shaft of light just ahead. They must be at the top. Sure enough, they all stepped back into the light of day. Johnny looked around. They were very high up and if it wasn't so foggy you could probably see for miles.

Trying very hard to ignore the cold, he turned to Oscar who was sitting on the rock balcony.

"What now?" he asked.

The answer he got made him jump. Tufty shouted loudly "RICKY, RICKY.. where are you, we need to talk with you. Ricky?"

Johnny looked around for Ricky. He shook his head. "Maybe he didn't hear?"

"No, Ricky always hears," said Tufty, winking at Johnny.

"Look!" Candy crowed.

Leaning over the balcony Johnny rubbed his eyes, thinking he was seeing things in the fog. He *was* seeing things. Things beyond his imagination.

Ever so slowly a boulder not far away seemed to move. Then to his amazement, a form was taking shape, getting bigger and bigger. Out of nothing, appeared a large stone giant. Having straightened up, it moved very slowly towards the pike till it was at eye level with the balcony. Johnny didn't know whether to be amazed or terrified.

Ricky really did look like a big pile of very rough-cut stone. Covered in various places with moss and grass, it was no wonder he blended in with the countryside. His eyes were deep set and dark and his face looked as if he had taken a severe beating. Johnny estimated that it would take six or seven of him standing one on top of the other to get to Ricky's size and with one swoop of a hand he could be crushed if so desired.

He looked at the troll's weather-beaten face. He didn't look quite as scary as Johnny first thought. The rough-hewed face was difficult to identify. To Johnny he just looked like a pile of stones, lots and lots of stones. If Ricky was a young troll, one had to wonder just how big adult trolls were. The other question in his head was how do rock trolls actually grow if they are rocks.

Tufty jumped up onto the ledge beaming. Glancing over the balcony at the drop, Johnny had to wonder if the squirrel was a little bit crazy. No way would he be doing that.... but then Tufty was, well ...Tufty. That basically described his friend.

"Gosh Ricky, you've grown heaps since we last saw you. We're terribly sorry to disturb you on this very cold day, but we need your help. An ice troll has kidnapped Dottie and we have to get her back before something terrible happens... like being eaten. Can you help us? Oscar has a plan."

Ricky leaned in towards the balcony and in a big booming voice greeted the group. It got windy every time he spoke.

Tufty introduced Johnny and Dog. Oscar was flapping his wings to get attention, there wasn't time to have the usual pleasantries, there was work to be done. His flapping got everyone's attention and all stopped and looked at the owl.

"Right, here is what I think will work. I've sent Candy up to the top of the pike to keep a lookout. We don't know where the troll is, so we are hoping you do Ricky. Once we have established that we can mount a three sided-attack, catch him unawares and grab Dottie...then run."

"That's not much of a plan" Freddie said.

His feathers ruffled, and Oscar glared at the mouse. "Well if you have a better plan, please feel free to speak up."

Just at that moment, Candy flew down and landed on the balcony. "Down in the next valley there are a lot of very dark looking clouds low to the ground.

"I think the ice troll is there, but it's hard to know for sure unless one of us flies closer to check."

"Right then, off you fly and hurry back." Oscar said.

Candy took flight and before very long was invisible in the fog. Everyone was quiet, waiting for her return.

When she came back her black feathers were all of a ruffle.

"He is down there and the very air around him is like ice," she said, panting. "There is a cage made of ice and Dottie is in there along with some other animals, it looked like a donkey or horse, a badger and a sheep. We definitely need a different plan to your one Oscar. I don't know how we can get them out of the cage, it is very thick ice."

"We need lots of rocks," Tufty pointed out. "In fact, Ricky, you are going to have to call up a lot of big boulders you can hurl and a pile of smaller ones we can. We can separate into two groups and attack together from either side. While he is fighting us, Freddie can run in unnoticed being small, probably unnoticed and get the animals out. Then, we just need to make sure we are all far away very quickly when the troll throws ice at us it can't reach us. Everyone will meet back here if separated."

CHAPTER EIGHTEEN

The war

They all went back inside the pike and down the stairs, Johnny holding the wall with every step. Much to his relief, he didn't see anything coming up whilst he was going down.

Once outside Johnny picked Freddie up and put him on his wooly hat to carry. Both birds were sitting on Ricky's shoulders and the other three started out at a brisk pace in an attempt to keep warm. Trampling over the uneven ground, crunching on ice as they walked, all kept their eyes down watching where they stepped. It wouldn't be nice to fall at this point in time.

The closer they got to the clouds ahead, the colder it became. Poor Dottie must be freezing, thought Johnny as he couldn't feel his feet here let alone be in a cage of ice.

Ricky stopped. Everyone else stopped. This would be where the stand would be mounted. Ricky opened his huge mouth and a very strange rumbling came out. It was quite deafening to Johnny who wasn't ready for such a thing.

He shouted, "What is Ricky doing, the noise will alert the ice troll?"

"He's singing to collect rocks, look."

Sure enough, as the troll sang his song, boulders started rolling towards him as he walked away. Huge boulders along with lots of smaller ones. He separated his hands and changed the tune of his call. Johnny stood and stared in amazement as the rocks separated into sizes, the small ones near him and Tufty and the large ones towards the troll.

What an indescribable picture it made!

Johnny wished he had a camera to capture the amazing scenery. At the same time worried that the ice troll would know they were there and be ready for them.

Soon he could no longer see the troll for the fog, but the rumbling song still filled the air. The song stopped suddenly. Then all chaos. There was the sound of rocks whizzing in the air followed by huge noises when they landed. So busy was he trying to work out what and where that it wasn't till Tufty yanked on his coat, he became aware the war had started.

He, along with Tufty and Dog, began picking up rocks and throwing them in the direction of the clouds. Freddie scurried down to the ground and took off at a run. Johnny was worried the poor mouse might be squashed by one of the many falling rocks.

Whilst everyone was occupied with the fighting, Freddie saw the cage and ran towards it, dodging rocks here and there. He stopped at the cage and looked in despair. The bars were very thick and he couldn't see a door or anything through which to get the animals out. The caged animals were huddled together in a corner trying to keep warm. They all were looking very frightened and miserable.

Dottie glanced at her friend and her soft voice almost broke with emotion. "Oh Freddie, I knew you would all come and rescue me and my new friends. I can hear crashing and much noise, but it's too foggy to really see what is going on. I don't know how you can get us out as there is no door.

"I know, I've looked. I'm going to go back to Johnny and tell them and hope they have an answer. I'll be right back," Freddie said, scurrying back over the snow the way he'd come.

Upon reaching the three warriors Freddie explained the problem. But there was another problem too. The ice troll was too big and the small rocks didn't do any damage and poor Ricky was struggling to fight the troll. Candy and Oscar were pretty useless in the fight as they couldn't lift big rocks. They were running out of energy and losing hope.

They couldn't rescue their friends.

CHAPTER NINETEEN

Ice trolls versus rock trolls versus dragon

A flapping noise alerted them to Oscar flying through the fog. He landed on the ground and the group updated each other. It appeared they were definitely losing the battle.

"I'm going for reinforcements," Oscar shouted above the boom of rocks and ice. "I'll be as quick as I can."

"What kind of reinforcements Oscar?" shouted Johnny. But he was talking to the air.

A new sound rang out. Ricky was singing a new song. It was even louder than before and sounded very scary. Just as they were trying to figure out what the new sound was, shapes started appearing out of the fog. More trolls!

Johnny thought Ricky was big, but this troll heading in their direction was twice his size. Johnny felt like an ant. A helpless ant at that.

"Whoa, now we're talking," shouted Tufty, jumping around excitedly. "Look Johnny, it's Ricky's family! They've come to help us. Now we can win."

Four giants were divided into pairs and each began a song. More and more large boulders started rolling towards them. They picked them up as if they were feathers and hurled them towards the ice troll. He was in turn hurling ice back at them in big chunks.

A lump grew in Johnny's throat. Now at last the friends saw a chance of winning.

One mighty troll picked up the biggest rock Johnny had ever seen and threw it at the giant. It hit the Ice troll's shoulder and he staggered trying to maintain his balance. Four more boulders flew at it and each one rocked the giant further and further away from the ice cage. The Ice troll was enraged at this point and being the size of the new trolls, picked up the pace of throwing ice rocks at them.

Suddenly, Tufty shouted. "Look Johnny, it's George."

Sure enough, their dragon friend looked to be coming to their rescue once again. The wind under his great wings blew the fog away and Johnny finally got his first view of an Ice Troll. Totally terrifying.

"Hurray!" they yelled loudly, jumping up and down.

No longer even trying to fight, they stood and watched events unfold. Five rock trolls and a dragon were a force the Ice troll couldn't match. It staggered again and fell. George was straight over the ice creature and heaved in a large amount of air, then released his fire. The fire covered the giant and – one minute he was throwing ice and the next, he was merely a large pool of steaming water.

"Hurray, Hurray" they sang and danced.

"You've done it, George."

Dog ran around in circles excitedly, as though chasing his own tail.

They all ran to the cage and told the group of animals they'd won. Now they just had to work out how to get them out of there.

Ricky's family had already disappeared into the mist and Ricky held a small rock by his standards in his hand, but a huge boulder by Johnny's. He dropped it at the other end from the animals, onto the cage.

The ice cage shattered and fell to the ground in pieces. Johnny flung his arms around Dottie's neck. Tufty and Dog were jumping up and down with joy.

George blew a small flame and created a campfire with which the frozen animals could warm themselves. There was a badger, a donkey, and a sheep. Introductions were made all around.

The badger was called Belle and lived in the woods at Calis Woods further down the valley. The donkey was called Jack and lived at the farm down in the valley along with the sheep, Tom. All were in debt to the group of friends; extending many thanks and promises to meet again, they turned and ran off towards their homes.

George sat and watched all his friends and knew he was the luckiest of Dragons. It gave him great joy to be able to repay them for saving him. He offered them a ride home the quick way which was received with a resounding yes. They all climbed on his back. Tufty stood up and shouted to Ricky.

"Thank your family for us please, we couldn't have done it without them. If it wasn't so cold, we would stay to play awhile, but I think we've all had enough adventure for one day. We will play again another day."

As the giant dragon took off and his wings spread, a chorus of grateful byes sounded in the valley. Then they were gone.

In the blink of an eye, they were back at the well. Compared to the place they had just left, the woods felt quite warm, but all agreed, even Tufty, that the best course of action now was to be indoors where it was warm.

Dog and Johnny set off back to the cottage, both ready for a warm fire and a cup of hot chocolate; and of course., there was still homework to do.

CHAPTER TWENTY

A birthday party to remember

Winter was coming to a welcome end and the ice was melting. Gone were the long dark cold days and nights and a new sense of freshness was in the air. It was a joy to be out and about in the sunshine.

The daffodils and bluebells were springing up throughout the woods and visitors were starting to come back. There was an air of expectation throughout Hebden Bridge.

The Wheelers had been at Cragg Cottage for 9 months now and everyone had gotten into a routine that worked well. The practice was growing in size and Johnny's dad was often working late. His mum also seemed more and more occupied with schoolwork. She had been offered the position of Headmistress and after talking it through with her husband had accepted the promotion.

As for poor Johnny, not much had changed.

School was still hard going. He had become friendly with one or two boys, but not so much that he thought to invite them over after school. His parents were so busy with their lives, neither noticed that Johnny still hadn't brought friends home. Sometimes it made Johnny feel sad and miss his friends from London. Other times he would give himself a talking to and remind himself he did have friends, friends who were very special.

Johnny didn't mind his parents being at work late, it gave him and Dog time to go for walks and explore, putting off the inevitable homework. By now he knew every inch of the woods and enjoyed trying to climb trees and skim rocks across the deeper parts of the river. He had even seen a flying fish or two.

It would soon be Johnny's 10th birthday and his mum had asked would he like a party. Secretly she was relieved when he said no, life was so busy it would have been a nightmare to organise.

The night before his birthday Tufty came knocking on the window. "Hi Johnny, come on, let's go have an adventure."

Not needing to be asked twice, Johnny slipped his feet into his slippers and climbed out the window with the squirrel. Faithful Dog followed suit.

They arrived at the well and the animals were all waiting, rather impatiently, for them.

"We have a surprise for you Johnny," Owl proudly announced. Even he had Tufty's excitement in his eyes.

Johnny didn't like surprises and knowing his friends, it could be any number of strange things. But, at the same time, he was curious. As they were at the well, he presumed they would be going that way and started to climb onto the well wall.

"Oh no, Johnny, we are going to the dam to see George," Dottie said, ever so gently.

"We're taking a different road this time," said Tufty, smiling.

So, off they set, the curious group of misfits, laughing and chatting in the middle of the night. What a beautiful night it was too; Stars were covering the dark skies and the moon was big and new. A perfect night for an adventure indeed.

They arrived at the river and took it in turns hopping the rocks across. Johnny carrying Dog in his arms and balancing on the slippery rocks to the other side. He was getting better at making it without getting his feet wet.

Once there they hurried to the dam wall and could see George already waiting for them.

Everyone got in a circle with Johnny in the middle. He looked around.

"So, what are we going to do?"

"Well," said George. "We know it's your birthday tomorrow so we thought we would have a special party for you. All aboard."

After everyone had scrambled up onto his back. George stretched out his magnificent wings and soared into the night sky. Flying over hills and trees, rocks and rivers, it was a magical experience. Like Aladdin on his magic carpet.

Shortly after, George started his descent, coming to land on an outcrop of rock.

Once on the ground, everyone jumped down. Over in the distance, they could see several outlines of moving objects. Johnny frowned, wondering what creature hid in the shadows this time.

When they got closer, Tufty yelled out. "Hi everyone, so glad you could make it. Look, Johnny, look who's coming to join your birthday party."

Sure enough, there was the badger, Belle. The donkey, Jack and the sheep Tom from their kidnapping adventure. To the left, sitting on a rock, glorious silver hair floating, sat Essy and her sisters from the waterfall. And, it took a moment to notice, but Ricky was also sitting there, so still, he blended in.

Johnny gasped and covered his mouth. He was truly surprised and happy. His chest filled with so much joy, he almost began crying.

"How wonderful to see you all," he cooed, excitedly. "I'm so excited. This is the best birthday ever. Thank you all so much for coming."

It was a marvelous party. They played games and sang songs. They took turns on George's back, splashed in the water with the nymphs and had rock-throwing competitions which Ricky was banned from for obvious reasons. Johnny could never remember another night like this and never wanted it to end.

"Everyone, hop onto my back, we're going to my cave under the dam. Oscar and Candy, Johnny will need to hold you, you won't have the strength to battle against the current. All aboard!"

Everyone scrambled up the dragon's back. The two birds settled in Johnny's lap whilst the others all re-arranged themselves so as not to fall off.

"Everyone ready? Here we go."

He stretched out his wings and rose gracefully off the ground, circling upwards till he was higher than the trees, and then he dived steeply towards the water. Johnny found it exhilarating, feeling the rush of air on his face and the sensation of flying free. Who needed human friends when he had these wonderful ones?

The dragon dove into the dark water without a splash. Down and down, he dove and yet Johnny didn't feel like he was drowning. In fact, it was bizarre how normal it was to breathe under the water. He glanced across and saw the others all seemingly, realising the same. They all shared a knowing smile.

After an endless descent, the dragon changed course and flew into what looked like a huge cavern. To everyone's surprise, it was dry inside. George landed and the group dismounted.

Looking up Johnny gave a gasp. The entire cave was filled with the tiniest of lights. Millions of them sparkling off and on.

"Wow" that was as much as he could utter, totally mesmerized by the lights.

Tufty stood next to him. "They're glow worms. You can only see them in dark caves, and they go out if startled. Your home is beautiful, George."

"Thank you, come let us go in and feast."

They walked further into the cave which seemed to go on forever. It split into two rooms and George led them into a second chamber which was decorated with enormous balloons and ribbons of every colour.

The table in the middle was overflowing with many strange looking foods. Johnny recognised the flowers from the waterfall adventure.

"Dig in," said George.

Not needing to be told twice, Freddie went straight for the dandelions.

Deciding to be adventurous Johnny sampled some of everything and to his delight, everything tasted like all his favourite things. The sound of laughter and cheer filled the enormous cavern so much it sounded like a hundred people were all talking at once.

"Speech!" yelled Candy.

A chorus of Yeses came back.

"Oh gosh, what can I say?" Johnny said, looking around. "My friends, I don't know how to say thank you. This is the absolute best birthday ever. I have come to love you so much. When we came to Hardcastle Craggs, I hated it. Now, I love it so much as I get to play and have adventures with you all. Nobody is as lucky as me.

"Thank you for a beautiful birthday adventure and the yummy food."

"You are welcome, Johnny, and we are so glad you came to live here with us too," replied Tufty, a big grin on his playful face.

All too soon it was time to go. They piled onto George's back and he flew them all back to the clearing. Everyone said goodbye and disappeared into the well. Johnny stood and watched till the woods were quiet and there was only Dog and himself.

"Let's go home and go to bed," said Dog.

They went back up the ivy and fell into bed, Johnny dreaming of all the magic of tonight.

At breakfast both his parents gave him a hug and kiss and gave him his birthday present.

It was a compass. "So, you will always find your way home," said his mum, giving him a hug.

CHAPTER TWENTY-ONE

New friends at school

At school, Johnny was expecting the usual lonely day. But Mrs. O'Brien came into the classroom with two children he'd never seen before. They were a twin; a boy and a girl.

"Class, please say hello to Christopher and Catherine Croft. They've just moved into Hebden Bridge so make them welcome."

The two made their way to the table in front of Johnny, both looking rather apprehensive.

Johnny started to smile. Maybe this could be a good thing, maybe, like him they wanted friends.

Sure enough, at lunchtime the two could be seen sitting alone. He took his tray and went to their table.

"Hi, I'm Johnny, can I sit with you?"

Their sad faces lit up. "Yes, that would be great," said the boy, downcast. "We don't think anyone likes us."

"Well, I know what that feels like, I've been here nearly a year and still don't have any friends. Maybe we can be friends if you like."

"Yes please," they both chorused together.

They all started laughing.

For the first time since the move, Johnny had hope. Maybe he can introduce them to his friends and they could all have adventures together.

Going home after school, Johnny had a skip in his stride.

Even his mum actually noticed and commented.

"It's nice to see you smiling, did you have a good day today?"

"Yes, some twins started today and we're going to be friends. Can I invite them over after school?

Sarah gave a heartfelt "absolutely".

CHAPTER TWENTY-TWO

The fellows of the wishing well say goodbye

That night, Johnny climbed out the window and went to the well with Dog. He called out for the others who all arrived in a matter of moments.

"Hi Johnny, you look happy," said Dottie the doe.

Johnny explained about the twins and finished by saying, "they can come on adventures with us."

The animals looked at Tufty.

The red squirrel cleared his throat and stood before Johnny with a mournful smile on his face.

"Johnny, we are so happy you finally have some friends. We can still remember your wish to the well for a friend to play with. Now, you have two. You don't need us anymore; your wish is granted."

Johnny scoffed and waved. "What, no, I do need you, I'll always need you."

Dottie came and put her forehead on Johnny's shoulder. "It doesn't work like that Johnny. When your dad was your age and he wished in the well, he wished for a girl to like him. That girl was your mum. When your parents got together, he didn't need us then.

"We said goodbye and were happy for him. He didn't remember all the adventures we had together. To him, they were just dreams he'd had. That's part of the magic... Now that time has come for you and we couldn't be happier. You will always be in our hearts and even though you won't remember all our adventures, you'll have dreams to remind you."

"It's time now for us to invite another lonely child, just like you were, to help them," said Oscar.

Poor Johnny started to cry. " No, that's not fair."

Freddie scurried up Johnny's leg to his shoulder. "It's ok Johnny, it really is. We are so happy for you and know you will be happy with real friends."

They sat for a while and talked of all the fun things they'd done together until it was time to go home.

With tears in his eyes, he hugged them all. He held on even tighter to Tufty. "Tufty, I'm going to miss you so much."

They all smiled. They knew he wouldn't remember in the morning, and that is how it should be.

He turned to Dog to say, "let's go home" and turned around one last time. The clearing was empty.

With a heavy heart, he walked home.

"Will you still talk to me Dog?"

"Not like this, Johnny, but I am going to be with you forever. We will just have different adventures and Chris and Catherine will be a part of them."

Johnny lay in bed and as he closed his heavy eyes, he smiled, heaved a sigh and drifted off into a peaceful sleep.